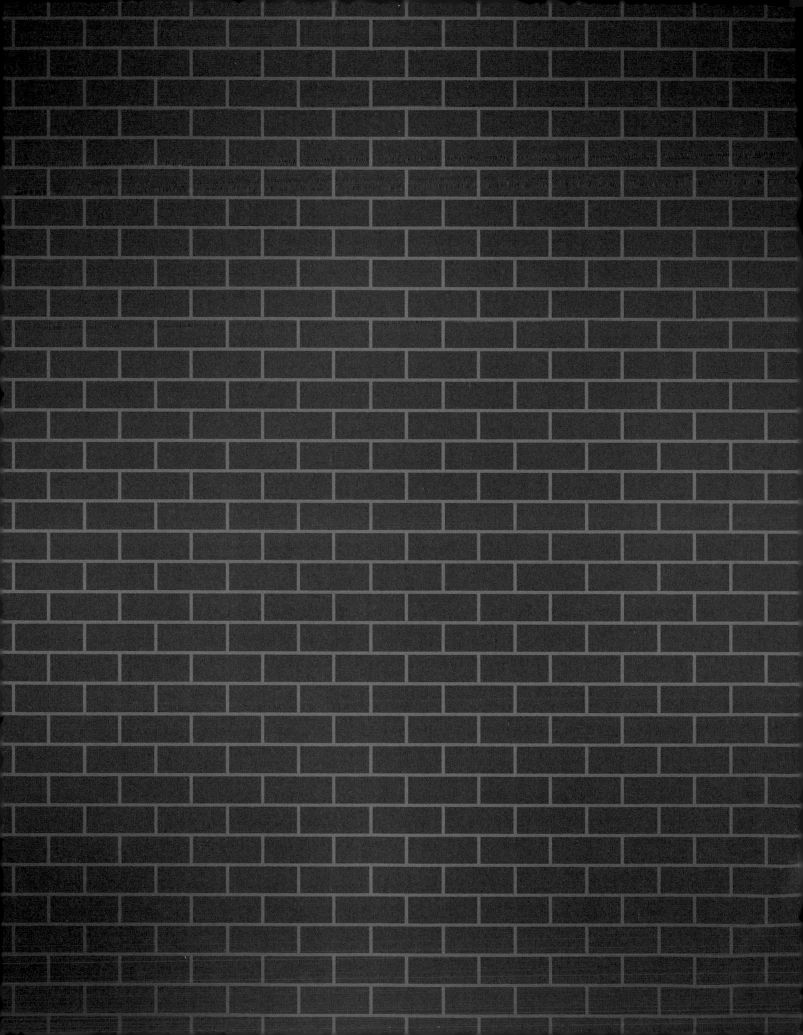

Adapted by Barbara Bazaldua
Illustrated by the Disney Storybook Artists

A GOLDEN BOOK • NEW YORK

ISBN: 978-0-7364-2954-2
randomhouse.com/kids
Printed in the United States of America
10 9 8 7 6 5

Wreck-It Ralph worked as the Bad Guy in a video game called *Fix-It Felix Jr.* Every time someone played the game, Ralph leaped on-screen and yelled, **"I'M GONNA WRECK IT!"** Then he climbed up the Nicelanders' big apartment building and pounded it to pieces.

Game after game, the Nicelanders called for Fix-It Felix, the game's Good Guy. Using his **magic hammer**, Felix fixed all the damage Ralph had caused.

The Nicelanders gave Felix medals and pie.

They threw poor Ralph in the mud.

The *Fix-It Felix Jr.* game had been in Litwak's Family Fun Center for thirty years. The game looked old-fashioned, but it still worked. Day after day, kids enjoyed watching Ralph wreck everything at the start of each game . . . and then had fun working the joystick to help Felix fix all the damage.

Inside the game, though, Ralph was
tired of getting thrown in the mud. He
wished he could win pies and medals,
like Felix.

**Why couldn't he be the
Good Guy once in a while?**

One night, Ralph traveled to another game
in the arcade to attend a support group for
video game Bad Guys.

When Ralph told them how he felt, the other
Bad Guys gasped. They believed that changing
who you were always led to trouble.

But Ralph was not convinced.

That evening, the Nicelanders held a thirtieth-anniversary party. But Ralph wasn't even invited. He felt terrible—wasn't he just as important to the game as Felix?

"I am going to that party!" he declared.

As soon as he got there, Ralph saw a cake with a candy Felix figurine on top, wearing a medal.

Ralph wanted his own figurine to wear a medal, too. But Nicelander Gene said, **"Bad Guys don't win medals!"** Ralph was so upset that he accidentally wrecked the cake!

Sadly, Ralph left and got a soda.
A dazed-looking soldier joined him.
He had come from a new game called
Hero's Duty. The goal of his game
was to battle nasty cy-bugs and
climb a tower to get a medal.
But when a bug ran across the
table, the soldier screamed
and fainted!

Ralph decided to visit *Hero's Duty*—
to win one of those medals!
He snuck into the game. At first,
it looked like his plan might work.
But once the game started, huge,
hungry cy-bugs attacked! They gobbled
up characters, vehicles, and weapons!

Ralph had never been so frightened! Luckily, the game was over quickly.

Inside *Hero's Duty*, as the game began to reset, a beacon appeared on top of the tower. The cy-bugs flew into the light and were

ZAPPED!

Sergeant Calhoun, leader of the soldiers, was furious. She yelled at Ralph for not following orders. But Ralph wasn't listening. He wanted the medal, which was at the top of that tower.

Meanwhile, a girl in Litwak's Family Fun Center
put her coins into the *Fix-It Felix Jr.* game. But
Ralph didn't appear on-screen. There was no one to
wreck the building.

"This
game's
busted!"

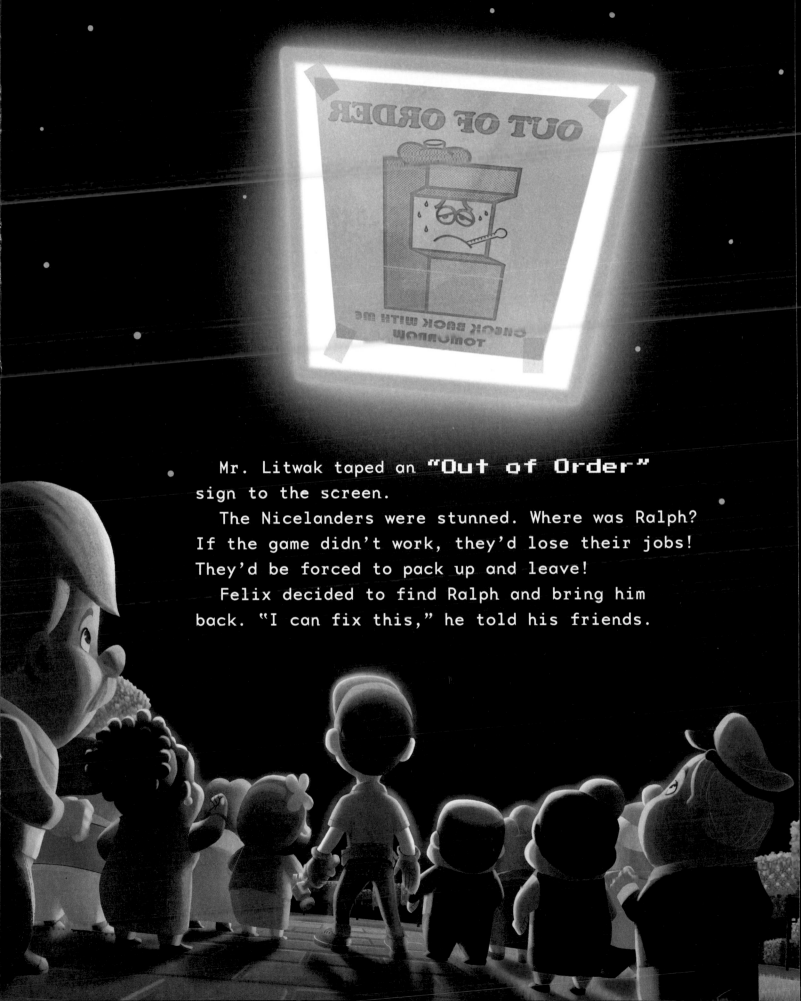

Mr. Litwak taped an **"Out of Order"** sign to the screen.

The Nicelanders were stunned. Where was Ralph? If the game didn't work, they'd lose their jobs! They'd be forced to pack up and leave!

Felix decided to find Ralph and bring him back. "I can fix this," he told his friends.

Back in *Hero's Duty*, Ralph was climbing the tower. After reaching the top, he tiptoed through a room full of cy-bug eggs. At last, he reached the Medal of Heroes. It was his!
Suddenly, his foot knocked an egg—**CRACK!**

A baby cy-bug emerged—and jumped onto Ralph's face!
Ralph tumbled into an escape pod, which
instantly launched from the tower.

Just then, Felix arrived in *Hero's Duty*, searching
for Ralph. He could see Ralph inside the escape pod as
it zoomed out of the game. But where was Ralph going?

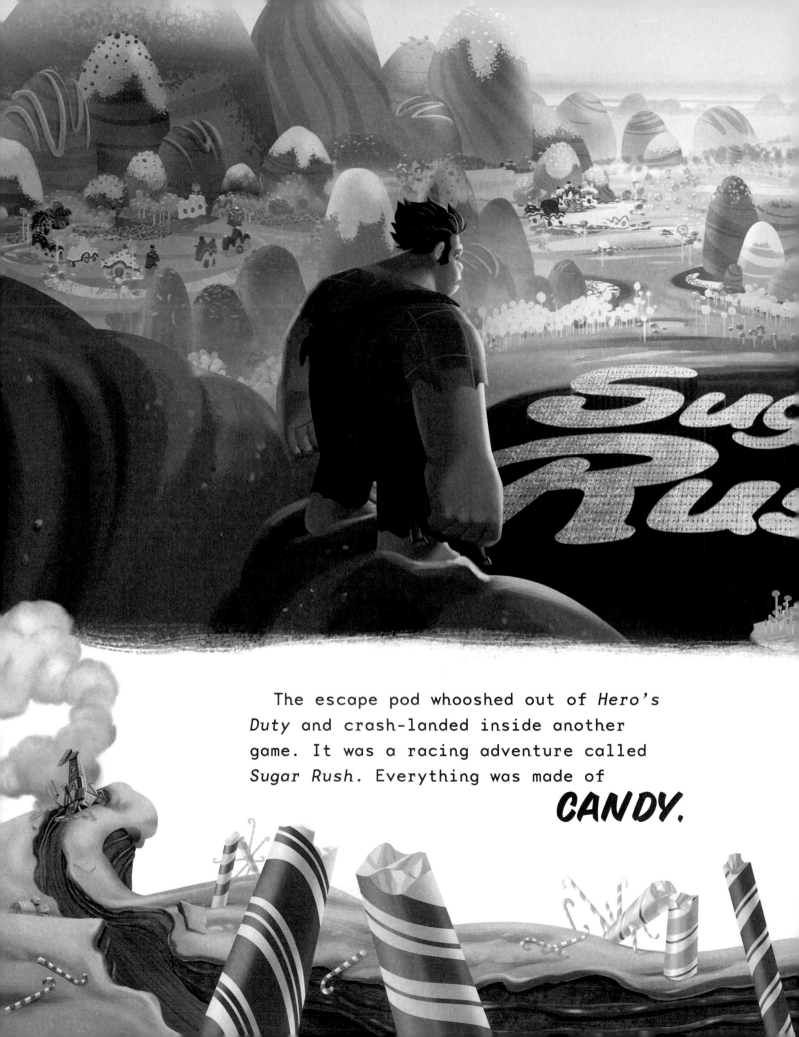

The escape pod whooshed out of *Hero's Duty* and crash-landed inside another game. It was a racing adventure called *Sugar Rush*. Everything was made of **CANDY.**

Ralph was thrown from the pod, and the cy-bug sank into a lake of taffy. The medal flew high into the branches of a peppermint tree.

Just th
covered i

Ralph tracked Vanellope through Lollistix
Forest. But just as he was about to confront
her, the other racers zoomed up.

They ordered Vanellope to drop out of the race. Then they smashed her kart and **TOSSED HER IN THE MUD!**

THAT MADE RALPH **MAD!**

He chased the mean racers away.

Vanellope thanked Ralph and promised
to return his medal if she won the
race. Reluctantly, Ralph agreed to
help her build a new kart.

With Calhoun's help, Felix found the wrecked escape pod.
Calhoun was worried. Even one loose cy-bug could
endanger all the games in the arcade. And Felix needed to
bring Ralph home.

"I don't want Ralph to **GO TURBO**," he told Calhoun.
"WHAT DOES THAT MEAN?" she asked.

Felix explained that Turbo had been the star of an old-style racing game—until a newer, fancier arcade game had arrived.

Turbo was so jealous that he left his own game and **snuck into the new one**.

People who tried to play the new game thought it was broken. Finally, Mr. Litwak unplugged both games and had them hauled away.

"I can't let that happen to my game," said Felix.

While Calhoun and Felix were talking, Ralph
and Vanellope snuck into the kart bakery and
used the equipment to bake a new kart. Gears
ground, flour flew, sugar spilled, eggs cracked,
and batter splattered!

The finished kart looked CRAZY . . . but
Vanellope

LOVED IT!

They took the kart to Vanellope's secret hideout inside Diet Cola Mountain. It was a huge cave with a stalactite of Mentos candy hanging over a lake of hot cola. Every now and then, a few Mentos would fall, sending up a fizzing plume of cola.

Ralph wrecked the rocks around the lake to make a practice racetrack. Ralph thought she might be a natural at racing—IF she didn't **TWITCH** and **GLITCH!**

Just before Vanellope and Ralph left for
the race, King Candy found Ralph alone. The
king had broken the rules and gotten Ralph's
medal back. He explained that if a glitch
ever won the race, *Sugar Rush* might be put
out of order—

FOR GOOD!

King Candy slipped away, and moments later, Vanellope arrived. With a smile, Vanellope gave Ralph a medal that she'd made just for him. It said

"YOU'RE MY HERO."

Ralph tried to talk Vanellope out of racing,
but she wouldn't listen.
Ralph felt terrible, but he really believed that
racing would put Vanellope in danger. With no other
choice, he wrecked her kart.

"YOU REALLY ARE A BAD GUY!"
Vanellope sobbed.

Sadly, Ralph
returned to the *Fix-It
Felix Jr.* game. All the
Nicelanders had fled.
He angrily hurled
his medal at the front
screen, and the **"Out
of Order"** sign
slipped off the glass.
Suddenly, he could see
the *Sugar Rush* console.
Vanellope's picture
was on it!

So King Candy had lied!
Vanellope wasn't a glitch—
she belonged in
Sugar Rush!

Ralph hurried back to *Sugar Rush*. Searching
for Vanellope, he discovered that King Candy
had locked her and Felix in his castle.
Ralph rescued them both and convinced Felix
to fix her kart.

Ralph, Vanellope, and Felix rushed to the stadium. The race had already started, but Ralph pushed Vanellope onto the track.

AND AWAY SHE WENT!

Vanellope sped up to the other racers. She glitched and twitched past them all.

"THIS IS MY KINGDOM!"

King Candy snarled, trying to keep his lead.

King Candy slammed into Vanellope's kart and started to glitch! As the crowd watched on the stadium's big screen, the king flickered for just a moment. He was really TURBO!

"YOU'VE RUINED EVERYTHING!" he yelled at Vanellope.

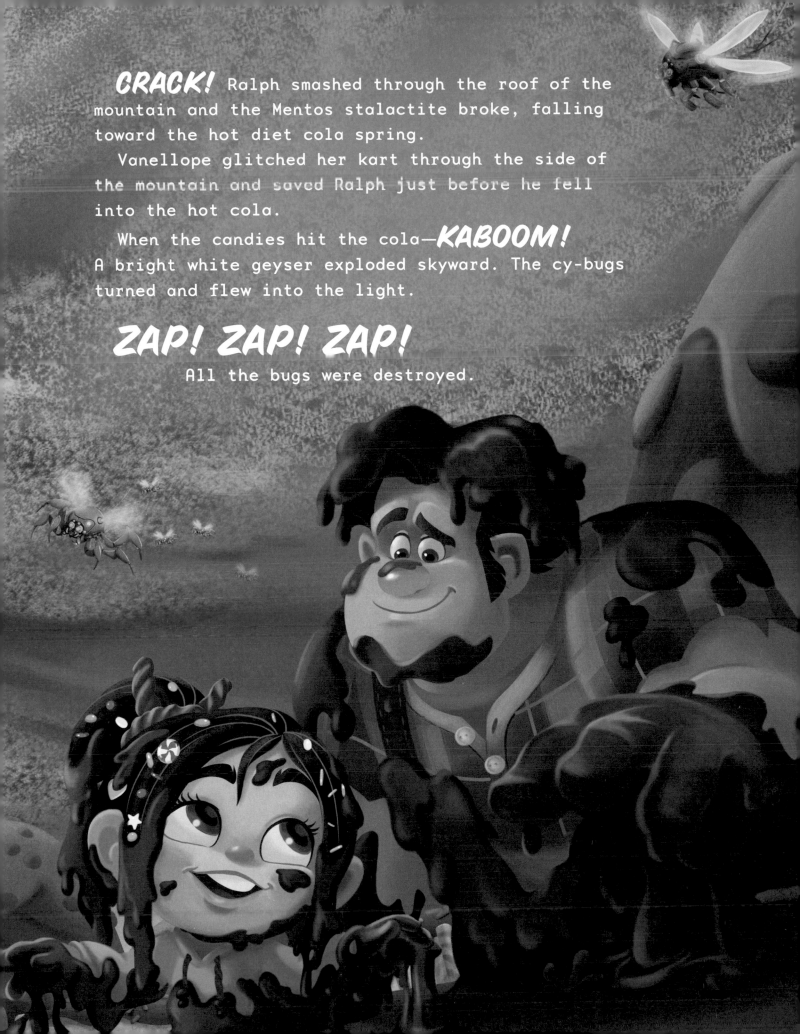

CRACK! Ralph smashed through the roof of the mountain and the Mentos stalactite broke, falling toward the hot diet cola spring.

Vanellope glitched her kart through the side of the mountain and saved Ralph just before he fell into the hot cola.

When the candies hit the cola—**KABOOM!** A bright white geyser exploded skyward. The cy-bugs turned and flew into the light.

ZAP! ZAP! ZAP!

All the bugs were destroyed.

With the cy-bugs gone, Felix fixed the finish
line, and Ralph pushed Vanellope's kart across it.
Immediately, the game reset. Then something
incredible happened: Vanellope began to sparkle,
and she was transformed into a

PRINCESS!

Vanellope was the rightful ruler of *Sugar Rush*.
But Vanellope didn't want to be a princess.
She preferred to be president! And she
really liked glitching. It was her racing
superpower!

It was time for Ralph, Felix, and
Calhoun to return to their own games.
Vanellope hugged Ralph

GOOD-BYE.

Back in the arcade, Mr. Litwak was just
about to unplug *Fix-it Felix Jr.* when
the little girl shouted that the game was
working. The kids lined up to play it.

Ralph was back, and **Niceland was saved!**

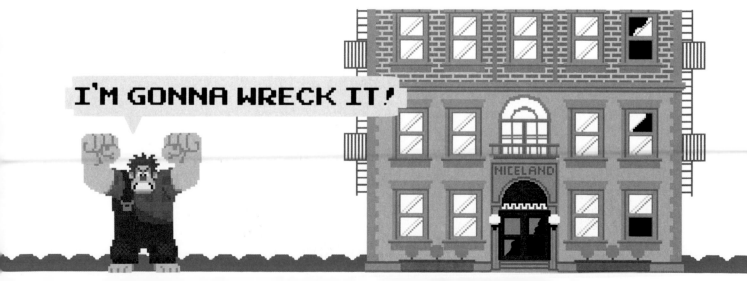

I'M GONNA WRECK IT!

Ralph still worked as the Bad Guy,
but he didn't mind now. The Nicelanders
appreciated him, and they even gave him
a special cake.

Best of all, Ralph knew he no longer
needed a medal to prove he was good.
**"Because if that little kid
likes me, how bad can I be?"**

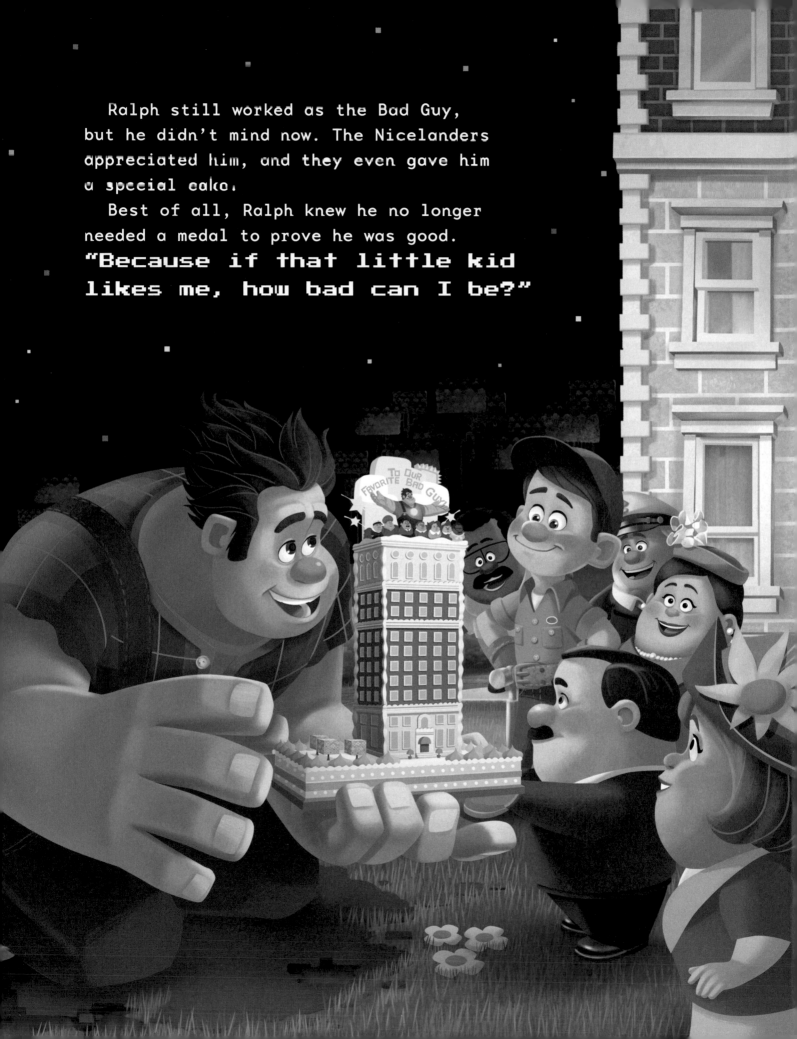